The New Kid

By DON PATTERSON

Illustrated by Sonny Schug

Hindsight Limited, PO Box 46406, Eden Prairie, MN 55344.

ISBN   1-929031-45-9
Library of Congress Control Number: 2002112581
Printed in the U.S.A.
First Hindsight ™ printing, November 2002

PICTURE CREDITS
Many thanks to the following organizations for giving permission to reprint illustrations and text used in the "In Hindsight" section of this book. The BBC WWII Home Life Interactive exhibit. The Imperial War Museum, London. Additional information courtesy of Alan L. Putland from *Remembering the Blitz in 1940*.

Written by Don Patterson
Illustrated by Sonny Schug/Studio West
Edited by Mary Parenteau
Production by Kline/Phoenix Advertising Graphics

To my daughter
Elaine.
You'll always be
my little girl.

TABLE OF CONTENTS

"THE NEW KID"

CHAPTER ONE

BIRDWATCHING

"Tag, you're it, Stuart!" young Harry Winslow shouted in a winded voice.

"I didn't feel a thing, Harry," Stuart scoffed. "You must have missed me."

"That's because he tagged you on your thick head," Stuart's little sister, Erin, hollered.

Stuart stooped over, as if to catch his breath. Then, a devilish grin flashed across his face and he tore after Erin and Harry. While the children chased each other, their playful shrieks of laughter carried over the fields.

Twelve year old Harry Winslow and his best friends, Stuart and Erin Bentley, enjoyed a warm summer day playing on a small hill in the pastures of Harry's family farm. The rolling countryside was always inviting, and this was their favorite place. What made the grassy knoll special was the view. On the other side of a bushy hedgerow fence bordering the Winslow property lay Hampton Airfield, home to a Royal Air Force fighter squadron.

Suddenly, the thunder of powerful engines echoed. Out on the neighboring airfield, twelve RAF Spitfires scrambled down the runway and lifted into the air. Climbing to altitude, the mighty fighter planes gathered in close formation and raced off into the distance. Harry and his friends stopped everything to watch, awed by the sight.

When the war in Europe first threatened England, two things changed in young Harry Winslow's life. His father was called away to serve in the British Intelligence, and the empty field next to his home was made into a landing strip for the RAF's 14th Fighter Squadron. Amazed by the pilots and planes, Harry quickly befriended the men, growing especially close to the Squadron Leader, Captain Ted Dawson. In his father's absence, Dawson and the others filled a particular emptiness in the boy's heart.

Harry tried to do as much as he could for his adopted RAF family, often assisting in ways well beyond his years. Stuart and Erin were eager to help as well. They savored the excitement of being around the squadron. When the children weren't actually with the pilots, they could be found waiting on the hilltop ready and willing to serve their heroic special friends.

Even with the 14th Squadron away, Harry, Stuart and Erin liked to keep an eye on the airfield. There was always something to see. Down on the hardstand, aircrews were busy repairing damaged planes and servicing new arrivals.

When a lone Spitfire landed on the field, the children dropped in the grass to watch. Visitors to Hampton were much more apparent in the absence of the squadron, especially to the spying eyes of Harry and his friends. They had become experts at identifying newcomers. By keeping a record of the serial numbers painted on the planes, sometimes famous pilots could be found. Working together, the vigilant young team had already spotted two well-known RAF combat aces in just the past month.

Harry clutched a pair of binoculars and focused on the arriving Spitfire, trying to read the numbers painted by the tail. Erin held a weathered scrapbook in her hands, and Stuart waited with pencil and paper to take notes.

"There it is," Harry mumbled. "It starts with a... W."

Erin leafed through her notebook filled with pictures of RAF airplanes, newspaper clippings, and pages of scribbled entries.

"Maybe it's Ginger Lacey!" she shouted, excited at the prospect of discovering a national hero like RAF fighter ace James "Ginger" Lacey.

"W..., 2..., 5...," Harry continued, struggling to follow the moving airplane and read the serial numbers at the same time.

"Harry," Erin demanded impatiently. "Tell us, W25 and then what?"

"Yeah, Harry," Stuart added. "Erin's right, if you can't read the whole thing, give us a look."

Amidst some playful shoving and grabbing for the binoculars, Harry pleaded, "Cut it out, guys. I can't see the rest until the plane turns. Besides, it's not Lacey, his serial number doesn't start with a W."

Caught up in the excitement of identifying the mysterious visitor, the children hardly noticed when Harry's mother stepped up from behind. In a gentle voice she asked, "Is anyone hungry?"

Stuart and Erin spun around. Mrs. Winslow pulled some fresh biscuits from a basket and waved them in front of the startled children. Tempted by the delicious offer, Stuart and Erin abandoned the game and clamored to her side. But Harry clung to his binoculars, determined to catch a glimpse of the last elusive serial numbers.

"Before I give you one, tell me what you've been doing all morning," Mrs. Winslow teased, and handed a biscuit to each of the two hungry children.

"We're birdwatching," Erin quickly announced.

Harry's mother looked up, surveyed the empty sky, and reported, "I don't see any birds."

"Not those birds, mum..., those," Stuart corrected by pointing at the planes down on the airfield. "We watch the planes and try to figure out who the pilots are. It's good fun."

"Oh, of course," Mrs. Winslow chuckled. "I'm sure it is."

While Erin and Stuart chatted with Mrs. Winslow, Harry continued studying the airplane on the field. Steadfast, he narrowed in on the remaining numbers.

"Children," Mrs. Winslow announced, "I have wonderful news. There's a carnival coming to town this weekend. I've made plans for us all to go."

"We can go to the carnival with you and Harry?" Stuart asked excitedly.

"That's right, dear," Mrs. Winslow replied. "I've cleared it with your mother so you and Erin can come along."

"Harry," Erin shouted, "we're all going to the carnival. Won't that be glorious?"

Still fixed on the Spitfire, Harry suddenly shouted, "I've got it! The serial number is W2535. See if you can find anything on W2535."

Erin quickly stuffed the biscuit in her mouth and scrambled back to her scrapbook. She raced through the pages searching for some record of the serial number. Coming up empty, Erin sat back on her feet and huffed, "Nothing."

The disappointed children eyed each other. This time, the visiting plane wasn't the mount of some famous fighter pilot. It was most likely just a messenger or replacement of some sort.

Mrs. Winslow sensed a lull in the action and seized the opportunity to try and pry Harry away from the airfield to have lunch.

"Come along, Harry, I've made a bite for you and your friends."

"But, Mom, the squadron isn't back yet," Harry impatiently complained.

Trying to strike a balance between her son's passion for the pilots and his need to eat, Mrs. Winslow offered, "I'm sure you can visit your pilots later. In the meantime, we'll make our carnival plans."

"Harry!" Erin begged. "We've been out here for hours and haven't eaten all day. Let's go with your mom and plan for the carnival."

"You go ahead," Harry replied, "I'll be there straight away, once the squadron lands."

Frustrated by her son's preoccupation with the airfield, Mrs. Winslow sighed, "Come along children. We'll have lunch and try to save him something, assuming he ever comes home."

With that, Harry's mother led Stuart and Erin back to the house. Mrs. Winslow worried about the amount of time Harry spent at the airfield. She couldn't help but wonder how much her young son was missing while watching and waiting for the pilots every day.

"Don't be too long, love," she called back.

"I won't, Mom," Harry shouted and then mumbled to himself, "I just want to be sure everything is all right."

CHAPTER TWO

THE DANGEROUS UNKNOWN

Flying twenty thousand feet above the choppy waters of the English Channel, Captain Dawson led his squadron home from an extended patrol. He couldn't help but breathe a sigh of relief when the coastline of England rolled into view. They had enjoyed the good fortune of an uneventful mission, but their Spitfires were low on fuel and the pilots were tired.

Suddenly, an urgent warning flashed through Dawson's headset like a bolt of lightning. One of his pilots, flying back in the formation, frantically called out, "Bandits! Bandits at three o'clock high!"

The veteran Squadron Leader glanced over his shoulder to search for the incoming enemy fighters. But, sunlight reflecting in the glass of his canopy practically blinded him.

Lost in the bright glare, Dawson couldn't see the group of German planes dropping from above ready to attack his RAF squadron.

Another warning sparked across the radio. Dawson recognized the voice of his friend and second in command, Captain Simms, counting out loud, "Seven..., eight..., nine of them. Closing fast!"

Seemingly out of nowhere, nine enemy fighters ripped through the formation of Spitfires with startling speed. Dawson instinctively rolled his plane to avoid a flash of deadly gunfire and quickly ordered his group to do the same.

"Break, lads! Break!"

Twisting and turning, fighter planes spilled out in all directions. Engine exhaust and con-trails traced white curling arcs against the blue sky as enemy planes stalked each other. Roaring guns filled the air with bright tracers and a hail-storm of bullets. The battle was on.

Captain Dawson's radio filled with a mix of frenzied messages to and from his men. They warned of danger and called for help. But, Dawson had his own problem. A German fighter had lined up on his tail. Preoccupied with evading the enemy determined to destroy him, there was little Dawson could do for the others.

The seasoned RAF Captain pushed at his controls and kicked his rudder, trying to escape gunfire from his adversary. Experience had taught him to anticipate the enemy's movements and use them to his advantage. Except, something was different this time. Somehow the German pilot was able to make his plane perform in ways Messerschmitt fighters had never been able to before.

For years, the RAF squadron scrambled to action in rugged Hawker Hurricanes. Only recently had their war-weary "Hurrybacks" been replaced by faster, more agile Spitfires. Over the last couple months Dawson had grown accustomed to the edge his new fighter provided over the German Me109s. Yet, for some reason, today he struggled to stay alive.

Spiraling through the air, Dawson ran from the stealthy German. The deadly chase etched curling trails of vapor all over the sky. Finally, he was able to cross back on the enemy fighter. Dawson triggered his guns when it passed in front of him. But, the sleek German plane nimbly dodged the stream of bullets and at full throttle sped out of sight.

Amazed, Captain Dawson realized he wasn't dueling with Messerschmitts. His squadron had stumbled into a fight with a group of something even more dangerous. Dawson shouted into the radio, trying to warn his men.

"Focke-Wulf 190s!"

The rest of the RAF pilots stiffened in their seats. They heard stories about the enemy's advanced fighter, but had never encountered them before. While combat was always hazardous, flying against new aircraft with unknown capabilities could have dire consequences.

The battle between the Spitfires and Focke-Wulfs raged on. Captain Dawson and his men fought valiantly, but the Germans seemed to hold the upper hand, enjoying the benefit of their new airplanes.

Suddenly, Dawson's radio flared with another alarming message, "They're all over Tate!"

Two of the powerful, snub-nosed German fighters pounded on Tate's Spitfire. The anxious lieutenant spiraled his plane earthward along a dizzying path, desperately trying to escape.

"I could use a little help here, lads," Tate radioed the others, trying to sound calm.

Captain Dawson hurled his plane in hot pursuit, responding to his Lieutenant's call. Quickly cutting in behind the Focke-Wulfs, Dawson fired his guns and drove off one of the German fighter planes.

"Tate," Dawson called, "I got one. Pull up to a stall and let the other cheeky devil pass under you!"

On his Captain's command, Tate pulled back on his stick, hard. The Spitfire lurched up and almost stopped in midair. Shocked by the surprising maneuver, the German pilot dove under the RAF plane and veered off into the distance.

The sudden brake of Tate's Spitfire may have saved it from the menacing Focke-Wulf, but at great cost to the pilot inside. The violent force from pitching up and down tossed Tate about the cockpit, knocking his head against the glass canopy. Unable to regain his senses, the dazed pilot sat helplessly while his plane began to twist and tumble through the air.

Watching Tate slowly spiral in a freefall,

Dawson called on the radio, "Tate, take control, lad. Tate..., you must take control!"

Dawson followed the failing Spitfire and continued calling to the injured pilot inside. Time was running out. Tate's plane was dropping through the air like a rock. Determined to save his young pilot, the Squadron Leader barked into the radio, trying to snap Tate out of his haze.

"Regain control of your aircraft immediately, Lieutenant, or I'll throw you in the stockade!"

Responding to either the volume or shear determination in Dawson's voice, Tate reached for the controls. The groggy pilot held fast to the rattling stick and started to kick at his rudder. Finally, by rolling the battered plane over, he wrestled back command of his wayward Spitfire.

"I'm on top of it," Tate radioed back, trying to shake the numbness from his head. "Just going to level out a bit."

Relieved for the moment, Captain Dawson relaxed in his seat. The rest of his squadron had managed to clear away the remaining Focke-Wulfs and Tate was still flying. The battle with Germany's newest weapon was over, without the loss of one of their own. They been lucky enough to fight to a draw. Hopefully, the experience and knowledge gained by the RAF pilots would help them next time.

"All right, gentlemen," Captain Dawson called to the squadron, "the excitement's over, it's time to go home. We have a lot of explaining to do."

CHAPTER THREE

AIRFIELD FOLKLORE

It quickly became apparent the German Focke-Wulfs had taken a toll on the 14th Squadron. Not only was Lieutenant Tate's Spitfire coughing smoke from a sputtering engine, the man inside was struggling as well. A cloud of concern followed the RAF pilots on their return to Hampton Airfield.

"Steady up, lad," Captain Dawson radioed to Lieutenant Tate in a matter-of-fact tone. "Keep your wings level, and your bearing straight."

"Roger," the injured Lieutenant weakly replied, "wings... level, go... straight."

The rest of the squadron remained silent while Lieutenant Tate's faltering Spitfire strayed in and out of formation, hardly flying level or straight. Captain Dawson shadowed the young pilot, constantly calling out encouragement and

correcting his course. When the green fields of
Hampton came into view, everyone quietly cheered.

"Andy, take the rest of the lads in," Dawson
ordered. "Land, and then clear the field. I'll stay
with Tate and make sure he remembers to lower
his landing gear."

Captain Simms nervously chuckled at
Dawson's attempt to lighten the tense situation.
As second in command, he understood the danger
of bringing in a damaged plane or an injured pilot.
A failed landing could be disastrous for the pilot
and the airfield. The best course of action was to
safely land everyone else first. Straight away,
Simms led the rest of the squadron ahead to land
at Hampton.

When the two remaining Spitfires finally
neared the airfield, Captain Dawson checked to
make sure the runway was clear of the other
planes. Tate's concussion blurred his vision, leaving
him entirely disoriented. Thanks to Dawson, he
had somehow managed to fly back to Hampton.
But, landing the lumbering Spitfire in his condition
would prove to be an even greater challenge.

"Tate, are you ready to head in?" Captain
Dawson asked. "Looks like they've cleared the

runway down there."

"Uhh..., yeah... sure, I'm ready," Tate mumbled in response.

Dawson and Tate were short of time, their Spitfires were practically empty of fuel. Anxious to land before the situation worsened, the Squadron Leader barked into his radio to get Tate's attention.

"Tate, look sharp! Line up on my wing. We're going to land."

Captain Dawson's terse command made Lieutenant Tate brace in his seat. Side by side, the two Spitfires descended toward the mouth of the grassy runway. As they neared earth, Dawson continued talking his pilot in.

"Landing gear down," Dawson called.

"Roger," Tate replied, "gear down."

"Full flaps and throttle back," Dawson continued.

"Flaps," mumbled the drowsy pilot, "and throttle back."

Captain Dawson's head swiveled back and forth, trying to watch Tate and land his own plane at the same time. As they edged closer to the field, a crosswind caught the Spitfires. Tate's wings started to tip and the nose plunged forward.

"Watch your horizon," Dawson sternly warned.

Tate had barely leveled his wings when the tires of his plane slammed into the turf. Constantly by his side, Captain Dawson's wheels gently settled in the grass at about the same time.

Lieutenant Tate's smoking Spitfire bounced down the field. Just then, his battered fighter veered right. The sudden change of path forced Dawson to quickly correct in order to avoid a fiery collision with the plane cutting in front of him. Dawson cleared out of the way, and Tate rolled to a stop at the end of the field.

Emergency vehicles sped to the crippled Spitfire. Instantly, a swarm of medics scrambled onto the wing of Tate's plane. Captain Dawson wanted to help, but could only watch while they quickly pulled the wounded Lieutenant from his cockpit. Moments later, an ambulance raced Tate off to the field hospital. Dawson knew his pilot was in good hands and joined the rest of the men gathered on the hardstand.

It didn't take long before the chatter between pilots reached a frenzy. Their encounter with the German Focke-Wulf 190s and near collision of the two Spitfires would soon become airfield folklore.

As the tall tales grew taller, the men could be overheard preaching the need for better airplanes and more experienced pilots.

Captain Dawson briefly glanced over his shoulder and noticed Harry Winslow standing in his familiar place on the other side of the hedgerow fence. The look in Harry's eyes told it all, he witnessed everything. Dawson waved at his young friend, assuring him things were all right.

Redirecting his attention back to his men, Dawson called, "Come on lads, off to the Briefing Room. Headquarters will want to know all we can tell them about those Focke-Wulf fighters."

CHAPTER FOUR

TIME TO JOIN

Harry Winslow ran all the way back to his house. He burst through the front door and shouted for Stuart and Erin. Mrs. Winslow rushed from the kitchen, worried by the fuss. Behind her followed his two alarmed friends.

"Harry, what's wrong?" Mrs. Winslow gasped. "Are you all right?"

"Yes, I'm fine," Harry exclaimed in a winded voice. "You should've seen what happened at the airfield!"

Stuart and Erin immediately started begging Harry to tell them what they missed. Comforted just to know her son was unharmed, Mrs. Winslow patiently corralled the excited children back into the kitchen to finish their lunch. Harry gulped down his meal while recounting every instant of the squadron's return, including a detailed description of the near collision of Spitfires.

"Well, I'm certainly glad it ended well and that everyone is safe," Mrs. Winslow concluded.

Then, changing the topic, she informed Harry, "While you were watching the squadron land, the three of us were busy planning our trip to the carnival."

"Carnival?" Harry asked, swallowing hard. "What carnival?"

"The one I mentioned earlier," Mrs. Winslow replied.

"Harry," Erin broke in, "don't you remember? Your mom is taking us all to the carnival this weekend."

"Oh, that," Harry replied, shaking his head. "Can't go. Captain Dawson is going to show me how to work the radio in his plane this weekend. A pilot needs to know his equipment."

Frustrated with Harry's single-mindedness, Mrs. Winslow scolded her son. "Harry, you're not a member of the RAF. You need to slow down, take a day off and enjoy yourself. The carnival will only be here for the weekend. It will be good fun, and we're all going. End of discussion!"

To emphasize her point, Harry's mother

dropped some dishes in the sink and stormed out of the kitchen. The three children timidly stared at each other, careful not to upset Mrs. Winslow any further.

Then Harry whispered across the table to Stuart, "The RAF needs pilots. I heard them talking about it on the hardstand."

Harry was devoted to his pilot friends. From shining their shoes and sewing their buttons to saving them from disaster, he was always there to help. Now, Harry was convinced he could give them what they needed most by joining the squadron.

"Stuart, you and I could help them," Harry urged proudly. "We should sign up today."

"You two... pilots?" Erin chortled.

"And why not, little Miss Smarty Pants?" Stuart shot back, excited by the thought of joining the RAF. "We know more about those planes than anyone else around here."

"Except for the real pilots!" Erin reminded them.

"Well, yeah," Harry stumbled. "But Captain Dawson... I mean, the RAF needs more. They were all saying something about needing better planes and more pilots, fast."

"I heard they've been taking most anyone who will sign up," Stuart eagerly added.

"Anyone old enough to know what they're doing," Erin corrected.

"No, Erin, Stuart's right," Harry argued. "They've bent the rules a bit. They'll take someone who's under age, with a parent's permission. I think now might be the time for us to join."

"Right," Stuart agreed, "Now is the time! Except, not today. I need to persuade my mother it's the right thing to do."

"Oh yeah," Harry confided, "I'll need to convince my mom, too."

Erin rolled her eyes and huffed, "You two are mad."

Stuart's younger sister knew it was ridiculous to think the Royal Air Force would ever allow twelve year olds into their ranks. More to the point, she knew her mother would never give Stuart permission before he turned eighteen.

"It's agreed then," Harry announced. "We'll get permission from our mothers and sign up with the RAF tomorrow."

Stuart gulped down the last bit of milk in his glass and bravely nodded, "It's agreed."

CHAPTER FIVE

THE SEND-OFF

Captain Dawson and the rest of the squadron gathered in the Briefing Room with a group of very interested commanders and intelligence officers. The pilots did their best to provide every ounce of information about the new Focke-Wulf fighters they encountered. And just when they thought they were finished reporting even the smallest details, they were asked to tell the whole story over again.

An officer asked Lieutenant Gainey if he remembered anything else important. The mischievous pilot, growing tired of the whole ordeal, replied, "Come to think of it, the plane hounding me had marks for four kills painted on it."

"What's critical about that?" the officer asked.

"Right from the off, I knew if he shot me down he'd be a new German ace," Gainey wryly announced. "That was incentive enough for me to make sure it didn't happen."

The room broke into laughter. Still, the need for information remained serious. The squadron had battled with the German Luftwaffe's newest weapon, and it was important to learn as much as possible. Any knowledge gained could be used to help the entire RAF.

Moments later, Colonel Harrison, the base commander, stepped into the room. Captain Dawson quickly excused himself from the fact gathering flurry of retold stories and joined the Colonel. He hoped to hear some good news on the condition of his injured pilot.

"I'm afraid Lieutenant Tate's concussion is rather severe," Colonel Harrison explained. "The flight surgeon feels it could be up to a month before he's able to fly again. I'm sending him off to Group 13 in Scotland for a rest. There's not much action up there. When he's better, we'll bring him back to Hampton."

Captain Dawson quietly nodded his head. He was relieved to know Tate would recover, but braced himself for the hard part. His job included informing the Lieutenant he was being sent away.

"When do you want me to tell him he's being transferred to Group 13?" Dawson asked.

"The surgeon says he's fit to travel anytime," Harrison replied. "Go help the lad pack his things, and I'll have a car waiting to drive him north."

Harrison left for his office to make the necessary travel arrangements. Meanwhile, Dawson found Captain Simms and explained the precarious situation. The RAF pilots were like family. Sending one away, even for needed rest, affected everyone. The squadron would sorely miss their gallant friend, on the ground and in the air.

Dawson drew a deep breath and headed for the door, ready to break the news to Lieutenant Tate. Stopping at the threshold, he looked back and told Simms, "Pass the word to the rest of the men. Prepare for a send-off."

Simms winked and nodded his head, then quickly went about telling the others. Moved by the serious condition of their fellow pilot, the rest of the squadron slipped out of the room and headed for the airfield.

It wasn't long before a pale and weak Lieutenant Tate stepped outside of his quarters, accompanied by Captain Dawson. The two men solemnly marched to a cab sent by Colonel Harrison. Dawson reached to open the door on the passenger side. When he straightened up, he found Lieutenant Tate stiffly standing at attention with his hand to his forehead in salute.

Captain Dawson eyed the frail pilot. Tate's service record listed him as just nineteen years old. But while Dawson studied the young man's drawn face, he realized how much the daily struggle of being a combat pilot had aged the Lieutenant.

"Chin up, lad," Dawson softly consoled. "You'll be back with us soon."

"Yes, sir," Tate replied, forcing a smile. "The sooner, the better."

With Lieutenant Tate slumped in the back seat, the car drove off. The injured pilot blindly stared out the window as the cab passed through Hampton Airfield's gate and rumbled down the rutted country way. He wondered who would replace him, and if that man would be good enough to protect his friends in his absence.

After several miles of twisting and turning through rolling pastures, the winding road straightened. Tate knew they had reached the border of Hampton County. A long trip north to the Scottish countryside lay ahead. The young lieutenant settled back in his seat. Resigned to being dispatched to the inactive northern air-fields, he closed his eyes and tried to rest.

"Lieutenant," the car's driver nervously interrupted, "why do you think those airplanes are following us?"

Surprised, Tate straightened up.

"Look!" the driver blurted out and pointed at the rear view mirror hanging in front of him.

Tate twisted around to look out the back and get a better view. The airplanes were pressing up from behind, flying barely above the tree tops.

"Tell me they're not German," the worried cabby demanded. "After all, you would know, right?"

Hurling through the air, the odd flight of planes roared over the top of the car and raced out in front of them. The frightened driver clung to his steering wheel while trying to watch the road and the planes at the same time. Amazed by the low flying formation, Tate counted eleven RAF Spitfires powering through the sky. When they turned, he noticed the squadron markings on

"It's my mates from Hampton!" *Tate shouted.*

their sides.

"It's my mates from Hampton!" Tate shouted.

The thundering Spitfires darted across the countryside and regrouped for another pass. Overwhelmed, the cab driver pulled off the road and squealed to a stop. Both Tate and the cabby jumped out of the car to watch as the squadron raced up the road and flew over again. Impressed by the display, the driver pointed at an empty gap in the otherwise perfectly spaced formation.

"They're missing one," the cabby remarked, confused by the apparent mistake.

"That's where I used to fly," Tate replied in a dejected voice.

As he spoke, the eleven remaining Spitfires of the 14th Squadron nosed up at full throttle and climbed high into the air. They passed out of sight an instant later, and the deafening engines faded into the distance.

The awestruck driver looked at Tate and said, "You must be something special for those lads to chase you down like that."

Tate quietly stared at the empty sky and whispered to himself, "No, they're the special ones."

CHAPTER SIX

"THE NEW KID"

Back at the airfield, Colonel Harrison provided a guided tour for a new recruit. After making arrangements for Lieutenant Tate to recuperate in Scotland, Harrison requested a replacement pilot be assigned to the squadron in order to keep them at full strength. The new flyer seemed young and fresh, especially in comparison to the career RAF base commander. His cropped red hair, youthful look and crisp new uniform made him stand out, even though all he wanted was to fit in with the others.

Colonel Harrison pointed at different buildings, sheds and hangers while explaining operations at Hampton to the new man. Making their way to the hardstand, they stopped to visit with some of the mechanics and crew. The nervous new pilot silently shadowed his Colonel's every move.

"Sergeant Pendleton," Harrison called to

Captain Dawson's maintenance chief, "have you seen Dawson? Or the rest of the squadron, for that matter?"

The stocky Sergeant stopped in his tracks. He was unsure of what Colonel Harrison would think about borrowing RAF aircraft and using precious fuel just to say good-bye to a fellow pilot. And with an unfamiliar stranger standing within earshot, Pendleton groped for the right words to answer the Colonel's question without divulging the Squadron's exact whereabouts.

"Captain Dawson is leading the Squadron on some... training maneuvers, sir."

"Training maneuvers?" Harrison asked, rubbing his chin. "What kind?"

"Ahh... formation flying," Pendleton delicately replied. "He took the lads on formation flying training maneuvers."

Harrison glared at Pendleton. A combat veteran himself, the Colonel was fully aware of his men's loyalty to each other and supportive of it. He leaned in close to the crew chief's ear and whispered, "When Captain Dawson returns from his send-off for Lieutenant Tate, do have him report to me. There's someone here I want him to meet."

Pendleton's face flushed red, caught in the unnecessary ruse. With a respectful salute, the embarrassed sergeant quickly replied, "Yes, sir!"

No sooner had Sergeant Pendleton finished, then the squadron of Spitfires thundered over the airfield, returning from their personal mission. One by one, the eleven planes smartly settled into the grassy turf. The pilots taxied to the hardstand in front of the maintenance hangers where they cut their engines and called for their ground crews.

Captain Dawson climbed from his cockpit and jumped to the ground. As usual, Sergeant Pendleton was there, greeting Dawson with a pat on the back and ready to tend to his airplane.

"I assume you ensured Lieutenant Tate is well on his way to Scotland," Pendleton knowingly remarked.

Nodding his head, Dawson replied, "That's right, Thomas, we sent the lad on his way."

A warm smile quickly flashed on Sergeant Pendleton's face, fueled by the bonds between all the men at Hampton. Focusing his concentration back to Dawson's Spitfire, the stocky flight mechanic asked, "Is there anything you need me to look at?"

Dawson dropped his headgear and tugged to release the straps of his parachute. "No, Thomas, nothing special. Just keep the squadron ready, including Tate's plane. There's always more flying to do."

"Yes, sir, I'll set the men to work," Pendleton replied, already signaling his mechanics to start refitting the Spitfires. "They'll be ready, whenever you need them. Oh yes, one more thing. Colonel Harrison would  like to see you, straight away. He's found a new kid."

Glancing across the hardstand, Captain Dawson spied Harrison and the new pilot waiting for him. While the Colonel seemed to be growing impatient, the new recruit was glad to bide his time watching the veteran RAF pilots and mechanics discuss their aircraft. Dawson collected his gear and made his way down the field to meet with Harrison and the replacement. When the young pilot saw Captain Dawson approaching, he stiffened up and cleared his throat, trying to make a good impression.

"Ah, Ted, come over here," Colonel Harrison

called. "I'd like to introduce you to our replacement pilot, Lieutenant Daniel Fitch."

Fitch snapped to attention. Dawson eyed the young Lieutenant. A head of flaming red hair instantly distinguished the new recruit. But what Dawson noticed most was his freckled face, shining with soft blue eyes and a hearty grin. To the hardened Squadron Leader, Daniel Fitch looked more like a schoolboy than a fighter pilot. Dawson immediately questioned the new kid's experience.

"So tell me, Lieutenant," Dawson asked, "how many hours of Spitfire flight training have you had?"

Lieutenant Fitch hesitated, trying to frame his answer. "In flight school we flew over 500 hours in Gladiators to earn our wings."

"Gladiators?!" Dawson snorted. "Biplanes like the Gladiator are extinct. I asked you about Spitfire training."

Fitch swallowed hard and offered, "I've logged over 100 hours of training in Hurrybacks. In fact, my flight school squadron even got bounced by Messerschmitts once. Only, our instructor ordered us not to engage."

Dawson studied the young pilot and shot back, "We used to fly Hurricanes, but our entire squadron was upgraded to Spitfires months ago. How much experience do you have flying Spits?"

By now the other pilots had gathered around Captain Dawson and Lieutenant Fitch. Captain Simms, Lieutenants Gainey and Hyatt and the other members of the squadron all wanted to get a good look at the new kid.

Dawson continued pressing the new recruit about his Spitfire training. A long, awkward moment passed before Fitch reluctantly answered, "Only ten hours, sir. But my instructor certified me as qualified for a squadron."

Dawson rolled his eyes and kicked at the ground, annoyed at being assigned a pilot with so little experience. In a huff, he snapped, "I'll determine who is and who isn't qualified to be a member of this squadron!"

Fitch anxiously held his breath at Dawson's stern reaction. Hoping for a little support, he searched the group of pilots for a sympathetic face, but found none.

"Andy," Dawson called to Captain Simms, "set him up with a headset and parachute. First thing tomorrow we'll take him up for a trial run."

Then Dawson turned back on Fitch, "It's simple, Lieutenant, you make it up there tomorrow and you're in. If you don't, you're out."

At that, Captain Simms gently grabbed the leery young pilot by the arm and pulled him away from the crowded hardstand. "Come along, Lieutenant. Let's get you fitted right. Then I'll show you to your quarters. You can get a good night's sleep in Tate's old bunk. Tomorrow you're going for the ride of your life."

Lieutenant Fitch followed Captain Simms to the supply building to pick up the necessary flight equipment. On the way to his quarters, the nervous new pilot dropped his headset twice while fumbling with the straps to his parachute.

Fitch followed Captain Simms like a dog on a leash for the rest of the day. The young Lieutenant tried his best to join in with the others, but without much success. Even though the pilots all seemed nice enough, they left him feeling a bit unwelcome. The squadron was like a family. For now they considered Fitch an outsider. They had no idea how desperately he hoped to find a home. Still, Captain Simms had a hunch about the new kid. He felt confident that if given a chance, Fitch would fit in just fine.

CHAPTER SEVEN

TOO YOUNG

Early the next morning, Harry Winslow and his mother sat at their kitchen table. While Mrs. Winslow poured over the newspaper, Harry reached for the sections she had finished. Practically every page contained an article about the war raging throughout the world. But, Harry was most interested in the stories about pilots and planes, especially ones with pictures for his scrapbook.

Suddenly, Harry blurted out, "Mom, I want to join the Royal Air Force. Everyone says they need more pilots."

Preoccupied with with her reading, Mrs. Winslow mumbled, "Yes dear, I'm sure you will someday."

"Mom, I mean now," Harry persisted. "Stuart and I made a pact. We want to join the

RAF today. He's going to get his mom's permission and then come over to our house."

Mrs. Winslow slowly folded the paper. Bewildered by Harry's abrupt desire to join the Royal Air Force, she stared at her son.

"When he gets here, will you take us to the recruiting office?" Harry boldly asked.

"Harry," his mother started to explain, "the RAF doesn't allow twelve year old boys to join. You and Stuart can't enlist until you're old enough. I'm hopeful there won't be a war when that time comes."

Harry sat up in his chair. "But that's the whole point, Mom. We want to help while we can."

Mrs. Winslow was proud of Harry's sincerity, but grew frustrated with his refusal to accept the limits of his age. Searching for a way to avoid an argument, she tried making her son feel needed by reminding him, "Harry, while your father is away, you're the man of the Winslow house. Without you, who will tend the farm for me?"

Harry shifted in his seat. He was stumped by his mother's question and lost for a reply. Quietly, Harry returned to the newspaper. The discussion was over and an awkward silence took its place.

A moment later, the thunder of fighter plane engines echoed from the airfield. Harry looked at his mother. His eyes telegraphed his thoughts. He felt embarrassed about not being able to enlist and wanted to get away. Mrs. Winslow simply nodded her permission for Harry to go and see his pilots.

Harry bolted out the door and raced to the airfield. He noticed Stuart and Erin up ahead, walking along the path leading to their favorite place overlooking the hardstand. Seeing Stuart reminded him about their agreement and his mother's refusal to let him join the RAF. Harry slowed down and quietly trailed behind them. He needed some time to figure out the best way to explain his problem.

When Harry finally reached his friends, it didn't take long for him to notice Stuart was in a foul mood. The three children silently trudged the rest of the way to the airfield. Eventually, Harry drew enough courage to tell Stuart the bad news.

"Stuart, I...," Harry stumbled, trying to find the right words.

"Harry," Erin interrupted, "before you say anything, Stuart has to tell you something."

Stuart nervously kicked the ground with the toe of his shoe, unable to speak. At last, he blurted out, "I'm sorry, Harry, my mom won't let me join the RAF with you."

"Stuart," Harry wailed, "my mom won't let me join either!"

The children eyed each other, flabbergasted. But the clumsy moment quickly passed.

"Did she say you're too young?" Erin asked, divulging most of the conversation between Stuart and their mother.

"That's exactly what she said," Harry shouted.

Stuart and Harry playfully shoved each other, drawn together by a common bond.

"I told you both," Erin chimed in, "there's no way our moms would let you join. After all, you're just kids."

The boys stopped their wrestling. Although Erin was right, they desperately wanted to help the pilots of Hampton by joining the RAF and were frustrated by being told they were too young.

Harry, Stuart and Erin continued down the path and finally arrived at the hill overlooking Hampton Airfield. As usual, they settled in behind the hedgerow and watched the crews going about their tasks. Everything seemed routine until an unknown pilot stepped onto the hardstand. The observant children quickly noticed the stranger. Spying over the bushes, they sized up the red-haired recruit. There was something oddly familiar about the young man on the field, and it wasn't his uniform.

CHAPTER EIGHT

THE FAMILIAR STRANGER

"Look at that, there's a new pilot out on the hardstand," Harry shouted, pointing toward the airfield. "Do you see him? By himself, over there, the one with the red hair."

Both Erin and Stuart nodded their heads and focused on the stranger. Erin found it curious that a new member of the squadron would be left to himself.

"He's new all right, but how do you know he's a pilot?" Erin asked. "None of the other pilots seem to pay him much attention. Maybe he's a new mechanic."

"No, Harry's right," Stuart added. "He's a pilot for sure. Mechanics don't wear parachutes."

Back on the hardstand, Lieutenant Daniel Fitch wrestled with his headgear and tugged at the loose fitting canvas straps of his parachute. The young pilot anxiously waited for Dawson and Simms to arrive so they could begin his qualification flight. Keeping to himself, Fitch felt relieved the other pilots seemed to ignore him. It made hiding his nervousness that much easier.

Fitch's world had dramatically changed in just one day. Fresh from RAF flight training, he was immediately assigned to active duty at Hampton. Even though the young lieutenant had been the top performer in his class at flight school, nothing had prepared him for the cold reception he received. He wanted to fit in and hoped Hampton would become his home, but everything seemed strange. The airfield, the squadron, and his commander were all new and not what he expected. The only things Fitch found familiar were the Spitfires.

"You might want to tighten the straps to your parachute," Lieutenant Gainey mischievously called to Fitch. "A 'chute's no good if you slip out when it opens."

Fitch's head snapped and his eyes widened at the alarming remark. Gainey brazenly stepped up to the stunned recruit and started tightening his straps. Lieutenant

Hyatt joined them, ready to pile on some more friendly teasing.

"Don't let Brian scare you," Hyatt started, offering a sarcastic consolation. "Remember, if it doesn't go well for you up there today, we could always use another mechanic."

Fitch quietly smiled and clung to his pride. He didn't mind a little ribbing from other men. The way he looked at it, at least they were talking to him.

Finally, Dawson and Simms arrived on the hardstand. The rest of the pilots, including Fitch,

quickly gathered around, ready to receive instructions from their Squadron Leader.

From behind the thick hedgerow fence, Harry and his friends watched the pilots huddle together out on the field. The children listened closely as Dawson assigned a number of tasks to keep the others busy while he and Captain Simms evaluated the new pilot's flight skills.

Harry couldn't help staring at the new recruit, convinced he had seen him before. He was just about to ask Stuart if he recognized the young pilot, when Erin mumbled, "The new guy sure seems familiar, doesn't he?"

"Yes," Harry exclaimed, excited at Erin's revelation. "I could swear I've seen him before, too, but I can't place him."

"Shhh," Stuart chided, "quiet down so we can hear what they're saying. Maybe we'll catch his name."

Captain Dawson finished assigning his list of small jobs and busy work to the pilots. As the rest of the men scurried to their tasks, Dawson and Simms prepared to get on with Fitch's flight evaluation.

"Lieutenant," Dawson announced, directing

his remark at Fitch. "I'm sure you would like to spend the morning getting to know everyone better, but there's much to be done."

The nervous young pilot straightened up and choked out, "Yes, sir."

Captain Dawson sized up the new recruit. Fitch's freckled face betrayed his youth. His service uniform fitted loosely, draping over the thin frame of a boy. Dawson had hoped for a seasoned veteran to replace Tate, but the reality of war meant replacements were generally young and inexperienced. Even though RAF flight training schools were expert at teaching fresh recruits how to fly, there was no substitute for experience when it came to survival. Staring at Fitch, Dawson wondered if the young man could handle a situation where lives depended on him.

"Very well," Dawson continued, concealing his concern. "Captain Simms and I will take you up and test your flight skills in a Spitfire."

"We'll even give you a chance to shoot us down," Simms added, giving Fitch a playful shove.

"You really want me to shoot at you?" Fitch asked, innocently.

"No!" Dawson retorted. "We won't even load

your guns until we're sure you know the differ-
ence between us and the enemy."

With that, Dawson
signaled it was time to go
and the three pilots walked
off to their awaiting planes.
The other men teased Fitch
along the way. Harry,
Stuart and Erin could hear
them from behind the hedgerow fence.

"Daniel," Lieutenant Hyatt heckled, "leave
your mum's number so we can ring her up if
anything goes wrong."

"I knew a pilot who survived his first training
flight with Captain Dawson," Gainey howled,
"and ten others who didn't."

Fitch held his head up, unflinched by the
taunting.

When Dawson reached his Spitfire he barked,
"You take Tate's plane."

Befuddled, Fitch looked around and asked,
"Which one was Tate's?"

Captain Simms gently grabbed Fitch by the
arm, "Stay with me, lad, I'll show you."

The remaining pilots gathered with the

aircrews on the edge of the hardstand, hoping to catch a glimpse of Lieutenant Fitch's qualification flight. Knowing Dawson and Simms, they would make it a good show for the audience crowded together on the ground.

Watching Fitch cross the field to his plane, Lieutenant Gainey, the youngest member of the squadron, elbowed Hyatt and whispered, "He must be even younger than I am."

"That's idiotic, Brian," Hyatt replied with a laugh, "the RAF doesn't take lads younger than you."

CHAPTER NINE

IN OR OUT

 Harry, Stuart and
Erin couldn't contain
themselves any longer.
They squeezed through a
small gap in the hedgerow
and raced to the airfield, eager to learn the identity
of the mysterious new pilot and excited about the
test flight.

On the hardstand, Lieutenant Gainey spun
around, surprised by the trample of footsteps
pounding up behind him. Instantly, the three
wide-eyed children posed a flurry of questions.

"Lieutenant Gainey," Stuart asked first, "did
the squadron get a new pilot?"

"Maybe. We'll see in a...," Gainey started,
but before he could finish, Erin interrupted with
another question.

"Where's Captain Dawson going with the
new pilot?"

"On a test flight to see..., " Gainey replied, but

was interrupted again, this time by Harry.

"What's his name?"

"Lieutenant...," Gainey's face suddenly went blank. "I had it a minute ago. It's... Daniel..."

Gainey glanced over to Hyatt, looking for help. Stumped, Hyatt stared back, shaking his head. Finally someone else in the group offered up, "Finch...? Or was it, Fish...? Something like that."

"Hopefully more finch than fish if he's going to fly against Dawson and Simms," Gainey smartly tossed back, and the crowd of men erupted in laughter.

The children didn't recognize the name, but they knew it was wrong, anyway. Harry couldn't understand why the squadron seemed so uncaring of their newest member that they wouldn't even know his name. He wanted answers.

"We overheard you teasing the new pilot," Harry revealed, looking straight at Gainey. "Don't you think you were a little harsh with him?"

The brash lieutenant stared at Harry and then shifted his eyes to Hyatt. In return, Lieutenant Hyatt cocked his head and shrugged his shoulders, but said nothing.

"A little harsh, you think?" Gainey replied.

"Yes," said Harry, "especially with him being a new member of the squadron."

Suddenly, Hyatt jumped into the conversation, "He's not a member yet!"

Harry was taken back by Lieutenant Hyatt's surly tone.

"Why don't you like him?" Harry asked.

Gainey fumbled with an explanation. "We all like him well enough. He seems to be a fine lad, but none of that matters. It's a life and death situation out there. We need to know if he's ready. We'd trust Tate with our lives. I don't know if we can do that with the new kid yet."

Then Hyatt took a turn. "Look, if he can't take a little teasing, he'll never be able to handle what he'll get from an enemy fighter. And for the rest of us, a timid pilot can be as dangerous as a German Messerschmitt."

"Or worse yet, a Focke-Wulf," Gainey added.

Nodding his head at Gainey's comment, Hyatt continued, "Captain Dawson and Captain Simms are taking him up to see what he's made of. He needs to prove he can be depended on in a scrap. When they get back, he's either in or out."

"Hyatt's right," Gainey agreed. "Soon enough,

Dawson and Simms will determine if he stays here with the family or gets sent back to school. We just need to be a little patient and watch it happen."

Harry, Stuart and Erin looked at each other. Respecting the explanation from their pilot friends, the three children joined the men sitting in the grass and prepared to watch the test flight.

Out on the field, Captain Dawson mounted his Spitfire while Simms led Fitch to Tate's repaired plane. Before the new kid climbed up to the cockpit, Captain Simms pointed to  a row of three victory emblems painted on the side, just under the canopy.

"Look, lad, Tate's already downed three Messerschmitts for you."

Fitch nodded his head, impressed by the previous pilot's tally.

"If you can get the two of us," Simms continued, tipping his head in Dawson's direction, "you'll be an ace."

Fitch smiled at the joke and hopped in the Spitfire. Nestled inside, he felt completely at home for the first time since his arrival at Hampton Airfield.

With a sudden burst of confidence, Fitch shouted to Captain Simms, "Would you prefer I shoot you down together, or one at a time?"

Simms grinned to himself. Trotting off to his plane, he called back, "That's what we're looking for Danny. Show us what you've got!"

Fitch grabbed the stick and tested the controls. His nerves calmed. He felt comfortable and capable in the seat of the Spitfire. Months of training had taught him all the necessary components of flight. This was what he had been waiting for, a chance to prove he was ready.

Suddenly, the radio sparked with an order from Captain Dawson, "Let's go!"

Lieutenant Fitch poured on the throttle and followed his two Captains onto the grassy field. The three Spitfires thundered down the runway and powered into the air.

Mastering his controls, Daniel Fitch felt entirely in his element.

CHAPTER TEN

QUALIFICATION FLIGHT

Captain Dawson, Captain Simms and the new kid, Lieutenant Fitch, soared through the sky in tight formation. Quickly climbing, the graceful Spitfires circled high over the airfield in plain view of everyone on the ground. Fitch checked his indicators in preparation for the qualification test, then briefly looked down at the patchwork of green fields below. The young pilot eagerly waited for the chance to prove himself and be accepted by the squadron.

Settling in the seat of his Spitfire, Captain Dawson eyed the gauges in front of him, noting their speed and heading. Simms and Fitch followed on his left wing, like members of a precision team.

"We've reached altitude," Dawson called into his radio. "Andy, you take the lead for maneuvers."

"Roger," Simms replied. "Time for some

formation flying."

"Okay, Fitch," Dawson continued, "when Simms calls to break, you follow his every move. I'll be behind you in the third slot... watching."

Captain Simms chuckled at Dawson's attempt to rattle Fitch with his overbearing tone. But, it had no effect on the young pilot. Fitch relaxed in the familiar surroundings of the cockpit. He calmly acknowledged the order and skillfully shifted his plane to the middle of the formation.

A moment later, Simms barked into his radio, "Break!"

The veteran RAF pilot rolled his Spitfire into a steep dive. Fitch followed, perfectly matching the lead plane. Dawson trailed behind and scrutinized every move.

The three planes dove, twisted, turned and climbed through the air, as if tied by string. From the ground, the precision flying of the Spitfires looked like a perfectly executed dance. The planes chased each other over and over, circling the fields of Hampton County. Eventually, Dawson ordered the pilots to level out.

Captain Dawson heaved a sigh of relief. He felt satisfied the young pilot could fly. In fact, it was obvious Fitch could fly well.

Careful to hide his opinion for the moment, Dawson coolly admitted, "Apparently the RAF has done an adequate job of teaching you how to fly, Lieutenant."

Now Dawson needed to know if Fitch was ready to fight. Lives depended on it. Before the young pilot could be accepted into the squadron, he had to prove he was prepared in all areas. The responsibility for making that life and death decision rested squarely on the shoulders of the Squadron Leader.

"Time for the real test, Lieutenant," Dawson commanded. "Let's see how you do in a dogfight. I wonder how long it will take for you to score a hit, assuming you even get a chance. When I call, break, come and get us."

Gaining confidence by the minute, Lieutenant Fitch smartly responded, "If I might ask, sir, which one of you would prefer to go down first?"

Captain Simms enjoyed the playful jab as

he quietly listened in his cockpit. In the world of fighter pilots, it was a good sign. Even Dawson felt bolstered by Fitch's new found nerve.

"Perhaps to even things up a bit I should give you a few tips, Lieutenant," Dawson shot back. "Always aim ahead of your target, and remember, surprise gives you the advantage. Next time we run into some Focke-Wulfs, we'll use surprise to break their formation and..."

Dawson's impromptu combat lesson was suddenly interrupted by the roar of Fitch's engine as he powered his Spitfire sharply away.

"Where's he going?" Dawson demanded. "I didn't order a break."

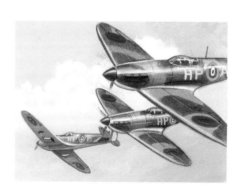

"You said break, Ted, and the lad jinked away," Simms laughingly replied. "Andy," Dawson argued, "I did no such thing."

"You did, and it looks like we've lost him."

Hearing the word, break, Fitch sped away, out of sight. Dawson realized the game was on, and immediately ordered Simms to follow on his wing while they searched for the young pilot.

The two RAF veterans circled the area designated for the pretend dogfight, wary of their young foe. They practiced some evasive maneuvers for their own protection and scoured the bright blue sky, ready to chase the new kid down. Suddenly, Dawson spotted the lone Spitfire passing above.

"Andy," Dawson called, "I see him at two o'clock high!"

Impressed by the young pilot's skill, Simms questioned, "How ever did he get there?"

"It doesn't matter!" Dawson snapped. "You circle high and I'll cross below. Force him down in front of me."

"Roger," Simms acknowledged.

With a burst of power, Captain Simms veered away, climbing fast. He swiftly directed his Spitfire to a position just above and behind Fitch. Then, Simms started bearing down on the young pilot, following Dawson's strategy.

Fitch worked his controls and kicked at the rudder pedals trying his best to evade Captain Simms. Dawson's Spitfire crossed under to cut him off and lined up behind him as well. Fitch was caught in their trap. Rolling over and over, the new recruit labored to shake the RAF veterans.

Abruptly, Fitch's radio sparked to life, carrying a nauseating message.

"Tat-tat-tat-tat-tat..." Dawson droned over the radio, indicating he had Fitch lined up in his gunsight.

Undaunted, Fitch quickly pitched his Spitfire up and climbed at a breakneck pace. Surprised by the daring maneuver, Simms lost position and had to break wide from the chase.

Captain Dawson tried to hang with the young pilot by climbing after him. But, Fitch started twisting his plane into a spin. Glaring sunlight spilled through the glass canopy and the flickering bright flashes practically blinded Dawson. Disappearing in the sunshine, Fitch brilliantly escaped his Captain.

"Andy," Dawson radioed to Simms, "I've lost Fitch. Can you find him?"

When the radio hissed with a return message, Dawson anticipated a reply from Captain Simms. Instead, the voice in his headset was that of Lieutenant Fitch.

"Tat-tat-tat-tat-tat," Fitch repeated over the radio in an annoying imitation of Dawson's earlier mock gunfire.

Startled by the sound, the RAF veterans found themselves in an unexpected situation. Dawson quickly glanced over his shoulder to locate the other Spitfires. Captain Simms was just off his wing, but Lieutenant Fitch followed right behind, stalking his every move. Hot on his

tail, Fitch singled out Simms and clearly caught him in his sights.

"Tat-tat-tat-tat-tat," Fitch repeated over and over.

Captain Simms immediately snapped into a

steep dive and flippantly called to Dawson, "I found him! Now I could use some help."

Lieutenant Fitch stuck to Captain Simms like glue. Fitch followed every move in perfect unison. Holding Simms constantly in his sights, the new kid playfully filled the radio with his sickening tat-tat-tat sound.

Captain Dawson hurled his Spitfire over in a race to save Simms from the embarrassment of being "shot down" by a recruit. Knifing in behind Fitch, Dawson aligned his sights on the Lieutenant's tail, and called into the radio, "It's my turn, Danny. Tat-tat-tat-tat-tat."

CHAPTER ELEVEN

THE REAL THING

Down on the ground, everyone watched the Spitfires circling above. Harry and his friends craned their necks following the chasing planes. The pilots studied the headstrong qualification flight even more intently. Their lives depended on the outcome. Wrapped up in the breathtaking display, the men jumped to their feet when Fitch escaped from their Squadron Leader. And when the young Lieutenant daringly lined up behind Simms, they all burst out cheering.

"Brilliant flying," Lieutenant Hyatt gasped in awe. "I think he's in, don't you, Brian?"

"Definitely in," Lieutenant Gainey replied. "He's family now. Just in time, too. We need all the help we can get."

"That's for sure," Hyatt agreed, gazing at the sky above. "Things might be looking up for all of us."

Opinions had quickly changed. Fitch more than qualified. He passed the test with a fantastic

demonstration of skill. Based on the chatter flying
about, Harry could tell the pilots all agreed. Now,
everyone seemed confident Fitch could help the
squadron and improve their chances in combat.
The three children joined in the cheering, excited
for the newest member of the 14th Squadron.

But the happy moment disappeared in a
flash. A formation of fighter planes, hidden in

the glaring sun, dropped on the three unsuspecting
Spitfires. Stunned, the pilots on the ground gasped
at the incredible scene unfolding above.

"German fighters!" Lieutenant Gainey

shouted, alerting the rest of the squadron. Grabbing his headset and parachute, Gainey called for the pilots to scramble, then raced off to his Spitfire.

Ground crews frantically dashed to their stations while the pilots dispersed to their airplanes. The pop of engines echoed across the field, and white plumes of exhaust quickly filled the air as the remaining Spitfires hurled down the runway. Powering into the sky, the RAF pilots raced to rescue their friends.

In the commotion, Harry, Stuart and Erin were left breathless on the hardstand. Harry desperately wanted to help, but all he could do this time was watch and wait.

High above, the German planes forced an abrupt end to the amusing game played by the RAF pilots. The three Spitfires were surprised by the attack and scattered to avoid being raked by enemy gunfire. Then, Dawson and Simms, the combat veterans, quickly regrouped around Fitch and prepared for a real fight.

Adjusting his goggles and bracing in his seat, Dawson radioed, "Try and keep them looking into the sun. Blind the devils, if you can."

"Roger," Simms replied, clearing the safety

away from the trigger on his stick. Guns ready, Simms keyed his radio and asked, "How many are there?"

Lieutenant Fitch's voice sparked in their headsets, "There's six of them, but they're not Messerschmitts."

"Focke-Wulfs!" Dawson shouted.

A squad of German Focke-Wulf 190s was flying a mission to goad RAF planes into a fight. Unfortunately for the English pilots, the enemy had stumbled onto their qualification test. Dawson recalled his last encounter with the new German planes. Yesterday, it took the whole squadron to drive them off. Today, they were outnumbered, two to one. Dawson suddenly realized it was even worse than that.

"Danny, get out of here!" the Squadron Leader yelled in an uncharacteristic panic. "You've got no ammunition. Your guns are empty!"

At the same time Dawson's warning flooded the radio, white hot tracer bullets arced past his plane. Amazingly fast, the Germans were already making another vicious pass on the small group of Spitfires.

Captain Dawson and Captain Simms boldly reeled their planes about and raced to engage the enemy. Bursts of gunfire erupted, filling the sky with flashes of bright tracers and deadly bullets. The two RAF pilots harassed the Focke-Wulfs as best they could, but were simply outnumbered. Worse yet, Fitch's guns were empty. He couldn't defend himself, let alone help his commanders. The young pilot's only option was to avoid the skirmish altogether.

Fitch reluctantly pitched his plane up and climbed away from the battle. Below him, the RAF and German fighters circled on each other like angry hornets around their nest. Then, one of the Spitfires suddenly bolted from the fray. Two sturdy Focke-Wulfs followed close behind it, guns blasting. The Spitfire's markings flashed into view. It was Dawson's plane. Fitch realized his Captain was in serious trouble.

Captain Simms also witnessed Dawson's plight. He cleverly escaped the other German fighters and raced to help his friend. Closing in on the fray, Simms thumbed the trigger to his guns and fired on the tails of the enemy planes hounding Dawson. Undaunted, the plundering Focke-Wulfs continued their hunt.

The dueling planes twisted through the sky. While Dawson raced to stay ahead of the two enemy fighters, Simms held fast to their tails and marked every move. Finally, the determined RAF veteran forced one of the Focke-Wulfs to break off. But, the cost of concentrating on one German plane allowed the second one to slip out of reach. The remaining Focke-Wulf fired relentlessly on Dawson's Spitfire, scoring hit after hit.

Lieutenant Fitch anxiously circled above, watching. He knew time was running out for Captain Dawson. Unable to just stand by and watch, Fitch searched for a way he could help. Suddenly, the new kid had an idea. The Germans didn't know he was unarmed. Perhaps he could scare the Focke-Wulf off Dawson before the enemy called his bluff. It wasn't much, but it was all he had.

Fitch threw his unarmed Spitfire into a perilous dive, willing to risk it all on his hasty plan. Crashing through the air, the young pilot held fast to his controls in a mad sprint to reach Dawson in time. Fitch pushed everything to the limit until he caught up to the Focke-Wulf stalking his Captain.

Fitch caught up to the Focke-Wulf stalking his Captain.

Hauling back on his stick, Fitch dropped in dangerously close behind the vicious German fighter. The resourceful RAF recruit adjusted the pitch of his propeller. By resetting the blades to the take-off position, the flattened prop sliced through the air faster and faster. While his thundering engine spun into the red zone, Fitch feverishly bucked his plane up and down precariously close to the German's rudder.

Fitch's fanatical flying and the deafening roar of his power pitched prop chopping at the air startled the enemy pilot. The Focke-Wulf snapped away from Dawson's battered Spitfire. It looked like Fitch's plan worked perfectly, until the German quickly circled back. This time, he lined up on the new recruit.

Lieutenant Fitch desperately hurled his Spitfire into another dive, attempting to slip away from the cunning German. When a line of tracer bullets ripped past his cockpit, the young RAF pilot realized he was still in trouble. The powerful wide nosed Focke-Wulf remained locked on his tail, guns blazing.

Defenseless, Fitch relied on all his flying skill to outrun the ferocious German, but to no

avail. The crack of gunfire grew louder and lines
of tracers seemed to flow in all directions. Then,
Fitch found himself surrounded by even more
fighters. The young pilot had never experienced
anything like this before and froze in his seat,
unsure of what to do next. Oddly enough, a vision
of Captain Dawson droning into the radio with that
annoying tat-tat-tat sound flashed in his mind.

Just when all seemed lost, the attack
suddenly stopped. The Focke-Wulf bearing down
on Fitch wheeled sharply away and raced out of
sight, as if in a panic. Confused, Fitch spied the
remaining planes around him. They weren't
German, they were RAF Spitfires! The rest of
the 14th Squadron had scrambled to the rescue
and cleared away the marauding enemy fighters.
The new kid escaped disaster, thanks to the
squadron's help.

CHAPTER TWELVE

A NEW MEMBER

Lieutenant Fitch wiped nervous sweat from his brow, relieved to see the Spitfires around him. Flying on the right, Captain Dawson waved at the young pilot and motioned for him to look to his other side. On the left, Captain Simms flashed a thumbs up sign from his cockpit.

Fitch was glad to see his commanders, but shuddered when he noticed a line of bullet holes ripped through the side of Dawson's Spitfire. He imagined his plane looked much the same. The young Lieutenant quickly realized how lucky he was to be safely nestled in the midst of the squadron.

Captain Dawson ordered everyone to regroup for one more patrol of the area. As the pilots took their positions, an empty space appeared where Lieutenant Tate used to fly. The Squadron Leader noticed Fitch's plane straggling behind and keyed his radio, "That includes you, Lieutenant Fitch. The empty slot is yours."

Daniel Fitch proudly smiled to himself, warmed by the confirmation he was officially a member of the squadron. He gently moved his Spitfire in line with the rest of the RAF planes. The other pilots grinned and waved at the new kid.

Dawson's full squadron circled the countryside in search of any remaining enemy planes. Once they assured the airfield was secure, the twelve Spitfires dropped toward the grassy runway and landed one by one. Safely on the ground, the excited pilots jumped from their cockpits and ran to congratulate Lieutenant Fitch on his flying skills. The happy band of men quickly huddled together and began sharing their stories, adding another page to Hampton Airfield's folklore.

Harry, Stuart and Erin stood in front of the maintenance hangers and watched the pilots make their way across the field. When the jolly group of men neared the hardstand, Captain Dawson buoyantly called out, "Harry, come here. I want you to meet someone."

The excited children raced to the boisterous

mob. Captain Dawson grabbed the new recruit by the arm and pulled him clear from the crowd.

"Harry, I'd like to introduce you and your

friends to Lieutenant Daniel Fitch," Dawson announced. "Our newest member of the squadron!"

The pilots all cheered. But when Harry, Stuart and Erin heard Fitch's name and saw the young redhead pilot face to face, they gasped. At the same time, Lieutenant Fitch gulped and held his breath at the sight of the three children.

Harry, Stuart and Erin had indeed met Daniel Fitch before. In fact just a couple years ago, the four of them used to play together on Harry's side of the hedgerow fence. Unexpectedly reunited, they silently stared at each other.

Before another word could be said, Captain Dawson interrupted the awkward moment by ordering, "Squadron, to the Briefing Room!"

The group of RAF pilots quickly headed off to discuss their second encounter with the German Focke-Wulfs. Trailing behind the others, Fitch glanced back at the three children and winked.

Their mouths fell open. Shocked by the sight of their old friend, Harry, Stuart and Erin dashed across the field and ran all the way back to the Winslow house.

The frantic children blew through the front door in a whirlwind. Harry shouted for his mother. Mrs. Winslow called back from the kitchen.

"Harry Winslow," she scolded, "you're always in such a hurry. What has you so excited this time?"

"Mom," Harry started, trying to catch his breath, "you have to let me join the RAF! They need all the help they can get. We heard them say it."

Stuart and Erin nodded their heads in support.

"Harry, love," Mrs. Winslow replied, "we've talked about this before, and the rules are clear. You must be eighteen years old to join the Royal

Air Force."

"Yes," Harry started to argue, "but if you have your parent's permission..."

Mrs. Winslow curtly cut him off, "That doesn't apply here. You're much too young."

Harry swallowed hard and yelled, "All we want to do is help, and you won't let us. It's not fair."

Frustrated with Harry's impatience, Mrs. Winslow exclaimed, "Just what is so unfair about making sure we don't send boys who aren't old enough to fight a war?"

Harry listened to his mother's objection, and framed his new found reason. He felt sure she would have to let him join if she knew there were other underage pilots already at Hampton.

"Lieutenant Fitch isn't old enough," Harry reported stubbornly. "He's not even sixteen, and he's a pilot."

"Who is Lieutenant Fitch?" Mrs. Winslow scowled. "And how do you know how old he is?"

"Mom, listen to me," Harry pleaded. "It's Danny Fitch! Remember the boy who stayed at Stuart's house a couple years ago? The one with the red hair? He's the new pilot in the squadron."

"It's Danny, for sure, Ma'am," Erin mumbled in support. "And he knew us, too."

"Flaming red hair on that one," Stuart chimed in. "Never forget that."

Memories of the red-haired boy jolted Mrs. Winslow.

"Of course I remember Danny," she replied. "But he's too young to be a pilot."

"Well," Harry announced, "today he became the newest member of the squadron. The three of us saw it all."

Stuart and Erin nodded their heads again. Mrs. Winslow dropped her hands on the table and stared at Harry. Thinking back a few years, she remembered when the Germans were poised to invade England. London and other cities along the coast were at the greatest risk of being attacked. Fearing for the lives of their children, many parents sent them to homes in the countryside to be out of harm's way.

Danny Fitch was one of them. At the time, he was a bright-eyed, freckled, sturdy twelve year old, with brilliant red hair. Stuart's and Erin's mother volunteered to take in the displaced child. Everyone got along so well, it was hard when the summer ended, and Danny returned to his home in the city.

Mrs. Winslow ran a quick calculation in her head. If it was true that Danny Fitch was the new recruit reporting to Hampton, the boy would only be fifteen years old.

"Mom," Harry shouted excitedly, "Danny just saved Captain Dawson's life. That's what I want to do. If Danny can join, why can't I?"

Mrs. Winslow kept staring, taking in all that everyone said. Then she quietly replied, "Harry, why don't you, Stuart and Erin run along and play. I have some thinking to do."

Minding her wishes, Harry and his friends ran outside and raced back to their favorite place by the airfield. Harry clung to the hope he may have persuaded his mother. Perhaps, Daniel Fitch had provided a way he could join the RAF, too.

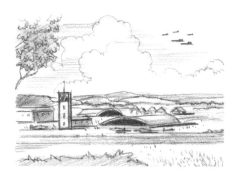

CHAPTER THIRTEEN

GETTING TO THE BOTTOM

Mrs. Winslow sat
quietly in her kitchen,
collected her thoughts and
reached for the telephone.
Dialing up Mrs. Bentley,
she hoped to get to the bottom
of the mysterious circumstances surrounding
Daniel Fitch.

"Helen," Mrs. Winslow began, trying to find
a comfortable way to start the conversation, "I
wanted to let you know, I've got tickets for the
carnival tomorrow. Harry and I will swing by and
pick up Stuart and Erin in the morning."

"That would be wonderful, dear," Mrs.
Bentley replied.

Mrs. Winslow added, "By the way, the children
just told me they saw Danny Fitch, the Londoner
who stayed with you a couple years back."

"Danny Fitch?" Stuart's mother repeated,
immediately recognizing the name of the boy who

stayed at her house a few summers ago. "Where did they see the lad? Was he with his parents?"

"Well, no," Mrs. Winslow stumbled. "It's far-fetched, but according to our children, he's a new pilot at Hampton Station."

"Danny? An RAF pilot at Hampton?" Helen gasped in disbelief. "That just can't be, dear. He couldn't be more than fifteen years old. How could he be an RAF pilot?"

Holding onto the telephone, Mrs. Winslow shook her head, unable to answer. The notion of it truly seemed absurd. How could the children be so assured he was the same boy?

"Perhaps the children were mistaken," Mrs. Winslow relented. "You know how they all look alike wrapped up in those uniforms."

"They sure do," Stuart's mother agreed. "Although, Danny would stick out. Even a uniform can't hide the lop of red hair on his head. Come to think of it, you could tell Danny from a mile away."

The observation by Stuart's mother touched off a flood of memories. Mrs. Winslow recalled young Danny's telltale red hair. It wasn't just noticeable, it was unforgettable. Harry, Stuart and

Erin played together with the red-haired boy practically everyday while he was in Hampton. Undoubt-
edly, of all people, they would know Danny Fitch if
they saw him.

"Helen," Mrs. Winslow finished, "I think I
need to make another call."

Mrs. Winslow hung up the telephone and
immediately dialed for Colonel Harrison at the
airfield. Explaining the situation surrounding
Daniel Fitch, she asked the Colonel to check his
records. Harrison respected her concern and invited
her to meet with him at his office.

Out at their favorite place on the hillside,
Harry, Stuart and Erin watched the airfield and
imagined what it would be like to serve in the RAF.
Erin suggested Danny Fitch should be their
commander. After all, it seemed he had paved the
way for children to join. Their daydream quickly
vanished when they noticed Mrs. Winslow walk
through Hampton's front gate and enter the
Operations Building. Anxiously, they scrambled
to get a better look.

The children crowded together in the grass
and nervously wondered why Harry's mother was
visiting. Then they saw Captain Dawson crossing

the field. The Squadron Leader briefly stopped for a friendly chat with some of the other pilots. Their cheery voices echoed loud enough for Harry and his friends to hear. Dawson continued on his way, and headed up the steps into the Operations Building.

"Ted, I'm glad you're here," Colonel Harrison announced when Captain Dawson stepped into the base commander's office. "Mrs. Winslow has brought to my attention a most alarming situation."

"Good day, Ma'am," Dawson politely greeted Harry's mother. "What's the problem?"

Mrs. Winslow put her hands on her hips and revealed, "Your new pilot, Daniel Fitch, is only fifteen years old. He's too young to be a fighter pilot."

"Lieutenant Fitch is only fifteen?" Captain Dawson doubtfully repeated. "Forgive me, Mrs. Winslow, but there must be some mistake. I know the lad looks young, but..."

"There's no mistake, Captain," she insisted. "Harry and his friends recognized the child."

"Mrs. Winslow," Dawson explained, "Lieutenant Fitch helped save my life today. I wouldn't call him a child."

"Perhaps not a child," Colonel Harrison broke in. "But, I'm afraid she's right, Ted. The lad won't even be sixteen for another three months."

Harrison stepped in front of his desk and recounted the whole story, "After Mrs. Winslow called me, I rang up Fitch's father. Apparently Danny's been bouncing around for some time. His parents first evacuated him  to the in-country fearing invasion a couple years ago. Then, the Fitch's lost their home in the Blitz. So they enrolled him in a boarding school while trying to resettle. In all the confusion, young Daniel somehow found a way to enlist in RAF flight training. His parents have been busy trying to put their lives back together, thinking he was safe at school. They had no way of knowing."

The three adults stood quietly for a moment, realizing the Fitch family had endured more than their share of hardship. The extreme circumstances surrounding young Danny were amazing.

Then, Mrs. Winslow pointed out, "The fact remains, he's too young. The RAF has no right to keep this boy."

"Mrs. Winslow," Colonel Harrison corrected, "the RAF has done nothing wrong here. Our policy is to honor the word of the recruit. Fitch stated he was eighteen on his enlistment papers, old enough to commit to service."

Both Mrs. Winslow and Captain Dawson looked at Colonel Harrison curiously.

"Nevertheless," Harrison finished, "upon investigation, the fact does remain that he is too young and his parents desperately need his help at home. He will be discharged immediately."

Mrs. Winslow clasped her hands in relief. Rightfully so, young Danny Fitch was going to be sent home for his own safety and to help his family resettle. After some polite farewells, Mrs. Winslow left, leaving the two RAF officers alone.

"Looks like I'll have to request yet another replacement pilot until Tate's return," Harrison sighed.

Captain Dawson nodded his head and added, "Hopefully, the next one will be old enough to shave."

Returning to the pile of paperwork on his

desk, Colonel Harrison barely cracked a smile at Dawson's wry remark.

"Colonel," Dawson interrupted, "do you want me to discharge the lad straight away?"

Harrison thought for a moment and then asked, "What is Fitch doing right now?"

"Celebrating with the rest of the pilots," Dawson replied.

Colonel Harrison carefully considered the situation before answering. "I don't see any benefit in rushing this. Wait and tell him tomorrow. Let the lad spend the night with the other pilots. We owe him that."

Outside on the other side of the hedgerow, Harry, Stuart and Erin stayed glued to the unfolding scene. When Mrs. Winslow stepped out of the Operations Building, Erin nervously grabbed Harry's arm. And when they saw Captain Dawson head for his quarters in a somber mood, she tightened her grip. The children realized Mrs. Winslow must have informed Colonel Harrison about Lieutenant Fitch. Harry's heart sank. He thought telling his mother about the new kid would help. Now, Harry wished he had said nothing.

CHAPTER FOURTEEN

PATIENCE IS THE KEY

Early the next morning, bright sun soaked the English countryside and a light summer breeze rustled through the fields. For the local villagers, it was perfect weather to start the weekend.

On the other hand, a gloomy mood hung over Hampton Airfield. The news of Daniel Fitch's age and his discharge from the RAF spread across the base like wildfire. The entire squadron of pilots solemnly gathered together out on the hardstand. They surrounded their new young friend and waited for the car that would take him home.

The squadron desperately wanted pilots that could be depended on to save lives, but not at the expense of those they were trying to protect. Even though Fitch had proven himself capable, it wasn't enough. Danny was too young by any standard. While he may have felt ready to serve, it would have been wrong to let him. The story of Danny Fitch, the boy pilot, was destined to go beyond Hampton Airfield folklore and become legend.

A cab pulled up, and Captain Dawson
reached to open the passenger door for his expelled
lieutenant. Captain Simms and the rest stiffened
to attention. Danny softly smiled at everyone and
slipped into the back seat. Dawson closed the door
while talking to the heavyhearted boy through the
open window.

"Danny," Dawson
started, "I'd like to thank you
for saving my life yesterday.
Remember, you'll always be
a member of our squadron.
Hopefully we'll end this war soon. But, if the time
comes when the RAF could use you, you'll be welcome
here."

Fitch looked around at the rest of the pilots.
To the man, they all firmly nodded their agreement.

"Here, this is yours," Dawson said, handing
Fitch an envelope. "Good bye and good luck, lad."

The cab slowly drove off to take Daniel
Fitch home. Alone in the back seat, Danny tore at
the envelope from Dawson. Inside was an RAF
service patch. It was the same one worn by
members of the 14th Squadron.

As the car wound down the rutted highway,

Danny thought about all that happened in the last few days. Being discharged from the RAF felt bittersweet. He already missed the thrill of flying with the squadron. But the farther he got from Hampton, the more he looked forward to seeing his parents again. Danny realized it was time for him to be with his family. Finally at peace with himself, he relaxed and settled in for the ride home.

The cab entered a straight stretch of road near the outskirts of Hampton County. Danny noticed the driver fussing with his rear view mirror and shifting in his seat. Concerned by the man's fidgeting, he leaned forward to ask the cabby if something was wrong.

"Look!" the cab driver shouted, frantically pointing out the window.

A formation of low flying Spitfires roared above them. Startled, the driver pulled over and stopped the car. Danny immediately jumped out to enjoy the breathtaking display.

The sleek RAF fighters gracefully circled to make another pass. When the planes turned, their markings flashed in plain view. Danny recognized they were from Hampton. Magnificently, his former squadron raced up the open road a second time and thundered overhead. Hurling past the car, the powerful Spitfires suddenly pitched up and climbed into the sky.

"They're missing one," the excited cabby observed, noticing an open slot in the formation.

"That's where I used to fly," Fitch mumbled, thumbing the squadron patch in his hand.

The awestruck driver eyed Danny and said, "Well, apparently your pilot mates think you're quite the hero."

Watching the squadron slip out of sight, Fitch quietly replied, "No, they're the heroes. I'm not old enough."

"Laddy," the cab driver explained in a fatherly fashion, "you don't need to be a fighter pilot to be a hero. You just have to be willing to help. There's no age restriction on that."

Danny Fitch clutched the patch in his hand. His face flushed with pride and a grin stretched from ear to ear. Climbing back into the seat of the car, Danny asked the gracious cabby, "Could you hurry me home? My family needs me."

"Straight away," the driver responded, steering the cab onto the road. "Let's not keep them waiting."

Back at Hampton Airfield, the 14th Squadron

roared over the countryside, returning from their special mission for Danny Fitch. The formation of eleven Spitfires circled the field and gracefully landed on the grassy runway.

 A sad Harry Winslow sat alone in his favorite place and watched. Nestled behind the thick hedgerow fence, he was practically hidden from view. The twelve year old boy preferred it that way. His mother had told him everything. She explained how Colonel Harrison and Captain Dawson admired Daniel Fitch, but agreed he was too young to be a combat pilot and needed to be sent home. Harry was angry with himself for revealing Danny's real age. The squadron needed good pilots and Fitch had proven himself worthy. Harry felt he betrayed his special friends and jeopardized their safety.

Time slowly passed for Harry as he aimlessly poked a stick at the ground. Lost in thought, he was startled when Captain Dawson suddenly sat down beside him.

"How are you today, Harry?" Dawson asked,

settling into the grass next to his young friend. A wave of guilt washed over Harry. He remained silent.

The painful hush spoke volumes. With a heavy sigh, the kindhearted Captain confided, "Mine's been a bit black, too. I spent the morning arranging young Mr. Fitch's discharge from the RAF."

Harry's heart ached. Watching the airfield day after day, he knew the danger facing his pilot friends. All Harry wanted to do was help, but this time things went wrong. His impatient attempt to join the RAF caused Danny's secret to be revealed. Now, short of pilots, especially a brilliant one like Fitch, the risk to the squadron was even greater. Feelings of rejection, frustration and shame gnawed at Harry's very soul.

"Harry," Dawson mentioned, "I hope you're not upset with your mother about Danny Fitch."

"My Mom?" Harry asked. "No, it's all my fault. I heard Lieutenant Gainey talking about how badly the RAF needs pilots. I thought if Mom knew Danny had joined, she'd let me. But, it backfired. Now you're shorthanded and I'm the one to blame."

Trying to work around any gossip Harry

may have overheard on the hardstand, Dawson explained, "No one's to blame, Harry. The fact is, Danny's too young. I appreciate everything you've been trying to do, but you really helped most by telling us about him before something terrible happened. We need as many pilots as we can get, but they have to be ready or everyone will suffer."

"But, what if the Germans attacked right now?" Harry jumped in. "What would you do without Danny Fitch?"

"What we always do," Dawson answered, "scramble our planes with the men we've got and do the best we can."

Harry worried aloud, "Danny saved you yesterday. What will you do without someone to protect you?"

"It's the risk we take," Dawson explained. "There's no guarantee. Not for me, Simms, Gainey or anyone for that matter. Our job is to protect children like you and Danny until you're ready. In return, all we ask is you do your best to prepare for the challenges you'll face when your time comes."

"I'm ready, right now!" Harry howled, trying to make Dawson understand. "I want to be a pilot so I can help. Why won't anyone let me?"

"Certain things can only come with age,"
Captain Dawson quickly answered. "Someday,
you'll be a pilot, or whatever you want. But, not
until the time is right. There's no use being in a
hurry to grow up, it happens at its own pace.
Besides, think of what you'll miss while rushing.
Find the balance between enjoying today and
preparing for tomorrow. Trust me, patience is the
key."

Harry stared at Dawson with doubting eyes.
In response, the Squadron Leader reassured him,
"Colonel Harrison will get us another replacement
soon. He'll fill in until Tate gets back."

"You're going to get a new replacement?"
Harry asked, hopeful at the thought. "Will he arrive
soon? I could help 'til he gets here."

"Harry," Dawson returned, "you've been
helping us ever since our squadron first arrived.
Hardly a day has passed where you haven't done
something for someone. Keep on caring for others
by doing the things you can. Right now, that's much
more important than being a pilot."

Harry smiled to himself. The advice from
his most special friend made him feel better.

Captain Dawson checked his watch, "I have

to get back to the squadron. This afternoon we can look at that radio, like we talked about."

Standing up to leave, Dawson spotted Harry's mother making her way up the path from the Winslow house. As planned, she was ready to take Harry and his friends to the carnival.

"Hello, Captain," Mrs. Winslow greeted. "What have you and Harry been up to this morning?"

Dawson winked at Harry and quipped, "Just some idle chatter between friends, Ma'am."

"Well, I'm sorry to interrupt," she replied, "but, Harry, we need to go if we want to make it to the carnival today."

Mrs. Winslow eyed her son. She anticipated an argument about leaving the airfield to go see the carnival. Ready for a fight, she was pleasantly surprised when, instead, Harry jumped up and exclaimed, "That's right, we're going to the carnival with Stuart and Erin today. I don't want to miss that. I've got to get ready."

Harry dashed down the path heading for home, but stopped short. Turning back he shouted, "I'm sorry, Captain, I'm a little busy today. Can we look at the radio another time?"

"Certainly, Harry," Dawson called.

"Whenever you're ready. There's no hurry, lad."

Mrs. Winslow glowed at the RAF Squadron Leader. She felt delighted to see Harry happy and acting like a boy his age. Grateful to have her twelve year old back, she took Dawson's hand and praised him, "I don't know what you said to Harry, but thank you. Thank you very much for everything."

With a gracious smile, Captain Dawson waved good bye and started for the airfield. He thought about Harry. His young friend was growing up fast, caught in a world at war. But, Harry was devoted to helping others. Practically everything he did was to the benefit of someone, one way or another. Dawson knowingly smiled to himself. He realized that while Hampton may have been short of pilots, Harry Winslow proved there was no shortage of heroes.

IN HINDSIGHT

"Older men declare war. But it is youth that must fight and die. And it is youth who must inherit the tribulation, the sorrow, and the triumphs that are the aftermath of war."

Herbert Hoover, June 27, 1944

As war with Germany approached in 1939, the British government took urgent steps to protect its population from the danger of air attack. Air raid instruction pamphlets were distributed, gas masks were issued to everyone (including infants) and bomb shelters were prepared. Also, plans were made for the mass evacuation of children and other vulnerable groups from cities. British officials feared their cities and large towns would be the primary targets of German air raids. Concerned for the welfare of those living in the densely populated areas, arrangements were made to evacuate children up to age 15, expectant mothers, the elderly and frail, hospital patients and the blind. It was believed homes in the countryside, miles away from any major town or city threatened by German bombing, provided the safest shelter

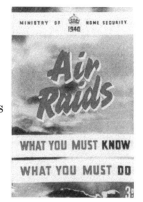

Air Raid pamphlet.

99

for these people.

Recognizing the capital city, London, was at greatest risk, the government encouraged families to evacuate their children and offered assistance to those who needed it. Many families left early, as was the case in other large English cities, but the majority of evacuees left London in a planned exodus starting on September 1, 1939. In just three days, over one and a half million people were moved to live with families in the rural countryside. One million of these were children, most of them traveling with their schools.

Parents were instructed to take their children to their school playgrounds, which became the evacuation assembly points. A large name tag for identification was to be pinned to the front of each child. In addition to bringing their government supplied gas mask, the recommended traveling items for evacuees were two changes of underwear, a warm coat, pajamas, a pair of socks, and toiletries including a bar of soap, toothbrush, toothpaste, towel, and comb or brush. Also, they were to bring a bag with enough food to last the day. Each child was allowed only the amount of luggage he or she could carry and no more. Many of them carried their suitcase, and had up to three bags hanging from their shoulders.

The school playground areas quickly filled with throngs of children and their parents. Mothers and fathers were promptly sent to registration lines alphabetically by name. As the lines of concerned parents and upset children grew longer, things seemed more chaotic. It was strange for everyone. Parents felt sad to send their children away, but hoped for their safety. While some children were frightened by the experience, others considered it a vacation of sorts.

Poster encouraging evacuation.

Teachers were given the task of organizing the evacuation process and were responsible for the children. They helped them register, assemble in groups and accompanied them to their destination. The teachers had the exhausting task of answering questions, comforting those who became upset, and controlling the disorderly. Once they boarded their transportation to take them out of the city, the teachers often acted as mothers and fathers to the children as well.

Extra trains and buses, all filled to capacity, were scheduled to accommodate the tremendous number of people leaving London during the three days of evacuation. Practically a million children, accompanied by their teachers left for the safety of the surrounding countryside. While efforts were made to keep most evacuees somewhat close to their home, some were sent as far away as Scotland.

Children loading in buses and trains.

Others were placed on ships to be taken to safe countries like Canada, Australia, and the United States. Sadly, several ships carrying those children were sunk by German submarines while attacking the convoys in which they traveled.

It was impossible to evacuate so many people, so quickly, without creating hardship. Parents gave up their children without knowing where they went until they arrived. Children were stripped from their homes and friends. And country families and the city children they took in often encountered stark differences.

After a trip consisting of numerous transfers between trains and buses, the children arrived at their destination and were selected by their prospective foster parents. Many of the evacuated came from poor families and knew little of anything outside the streets of their own neighborhood. Life in the confines of the city was drastically different from life in the open pastures of the countryside, especially with new foster parents who were total strangers. Being an evacuee was an adventure for many children who had never seen the country before. Others were homesick and unhappy in their foster homes.

When the expected air raids didn't happen in the early months of the war, approximately half the evacuees returned to their homes. But, many were later re-evacuated when Germany started its air assault on London during the Blitz in late 1940 and again, when the V1 and V2 rocket bomb attacks began in 1944. By early 1945, allied forces were liberating countries on the European mainland and closing in on Germany. The end of the war was in sight, and almost all evacuees had returned home.

GLOSSARY

Ace: A pilot with five confirmed victories.

Biplanes: Early aircraft with two wings, one fixed above and one below the fuselage. Primarily used in World War I.

Black: English term meaning bad.

Captain: A military officer ranking below colonel and above lieutenant.

Colonel: A military officer ranking below general and above captain.

Contrails: Streaks of condensed water vapor created by aircraft at high altitudes (condensation trail).

Enlist: Joining the military service.

Focke-Wulf 190: A German fighter plane (also Focke-Wulf).

Formation: Aircraft flying together in unison or in a specific configuration, such as a row straight across or aligned in a V.

Fuselage: The central body of an airplane.

Hardstand: A hard surfaced area next to an airstrip used for parking planes and ground vehicles.

Hawker Hurricane: A type of British fighter plane (also called "Hurrybacks" by RAF pilots).

Hedgerow: A row of bushes or small trees that form a fence.

Jink Away: RAF term for a sudden evasive action or maneuver.

Lieutenant: A military officer ranking below captain.

Messerschmitt 109: A type of German fighter plane (also Me 109).

Operations Building: The airfield's central administration building.

Propeller Pitch: Propeller blades could be adjusted to variable angles (pitch) to create more power or speed.

Scramble: The immediate launch of airplanes from the airfield.

Serial Number: An identification number specific to each airplane.

Stick or Yoke: The control stick of an airplane used for steering.

Supermarine Spitfire: A type of British fighter plane (also Spit).